RISE OF THE
ZOMBIE RABBIT

For Alice and Archie,
funny bunnies—SH

For Freya and Rhiannon—SC

GROSSET & DUNLAP
Penguin Young Readers Group
An Imprint of Penguin Random House LLC

Text copyright © 2013 by Sam Hay. Illustrations copyright © 2013 by Simon Cooper. All rights reserved.
First printed in Great Britain in 2013 by Stripes Publishing. First published in the United States in 2015 by
Grosset & Dunlap, an imprint of Penguin Random House LLC, 345 Hudson Street,
New York, New York 10014. GROSSET & DUNLAP is a trademark of
Penguin Random House LLC. Printed in the USA.

Library of Congress Cataloging-in-Publication Data is available.

ISBN 978-0-448-47799-2   10 9 8 7 6 5 4 3 2 1

UNDEAD PETS

RISE OF THE ZOMBIE RABBIT

by Sam Hay

illustrated by Simon Cooper

Grosset & Dunlap
An Imprint of Penguin Random House

The story so far . . .

Ten-year-old Joe Edmunds is desperate for a pet.

But his mom's allergies mean that he's got no chance.

Then his great-uncle Charlie gives him an ancient Egyptian amulet that he claims will grant Joe a single wish . . .

But instead of getting a pet, Joe becomes the Protector of Undead Pets.
He is bound by the amulet to solve the problems of zombie pets so
they can pass peacefully to the afterlife.

And so the
trouble begins . . .

CHAPTER ONE

Joe peeked around the stage curtain and gasped. "Wow! It's packed. Look, Matt!" He nudged his best friend, who was busy digging inside an old top hat.

"I'm sure I put the flowers in here," Matt said, turning the hat upside down and giving it a thump.

It was Friday night, and families and friends were jammed into the school's auditorium to watch the kids compete in the sixth-grade talent show. Joe could see his mom and dad and his little brother, Toby, in the front row. His sister, Sarah, had gone to a friend's house for the night instead. Toby was leaning forward, his eyes glued to the stage. He couldn't wait to see Joe and Matt's magic act. They'd been practicing for weeks.

"Joe, where'd the knotted string go?" asked Matt, patting his coat pockets nervously.

"I've got it here," Joe said, holding it up. "Stop worrying, Matt!"

Their principal, Mr. Hill, swept past with a clipboard in his hands. "Five minutes to curtain!" he called. "Form a line in the order you're going onstage, please."

As he spoke, the stage lights flickered eerily above their heads.

"Oooooooooooh!" The children giggled.

"Oh no!" groaned Mr. Hill. "The last thing we need is a power outage."

"Must be the wind," said Nick the Stick, the tallest boy in Joe's class. "It's blowing hard out there—a tree branch nearly hit our car on the way here."

As he spoke, Nick was spinning a basketball around and around on one finger.

Joe and Matt exchanged a look. Nick was amazing at ball tricks. As well as being the basketball king of the school, he could roll a ball down his back and flick it back up over his head.

"We'll never beat Nick's basketball routine," said Matt. "And look—there's the twins' dog! They've trained her to do tricks."

Smartie the dog was doing a routine with her owners, Ava and Molly—two girls in Joe's class. A little further back, Joe could see Spiker and Harry practicing their yo-yo moves. In the corner, another group from Joe's class was warming up for a gymnastics act.

Mr. Hill looked around. "Where are Leonie and Natalie?" He peered at his clipboard. "They're supposed to be the first act."

Mr. Hill looked over at Joe and Matt. "If they're not here soon, you two will have to go on first."

"What?" squeaked Matt. "I'm not ready yet! Joe, have we got all the props?"

"Yes! Check your pockets. They're definitely in there. We already went through everything, remember?"

Both boys were wearing long, dark overcoats with deep pockets and wide sleeves, perfect for hiding things—and losing them! Joe had borrowed his coat from his granddad. It was a bit big and smelled of pickled onions, but Joe thought it made him look mysterious.

"Ta-da!" said Matt suddenly. He produced a squashed bunch of paper flowers from up his sleeve.

"What about the rabbit?" asked Joe. It was one of their best tricks—pulling a cuddly toy bunny out of a seemingly empty top hat. "Is it definitely in there?"

Matt nodded. "Yeah, it's hidden at the bottom."

"One minute to curtain!" called Mr. Hill. "If Leonie and Natalie don't appear in the next ten seconds, you boys will have to go on first."

"We're here!" wailed Leonie, clambering up the steps in a pair of bright red shoes. Natalie was right behind her. "We were just having a last-minute practice!"

Just then, the sound of piano music rang out from the front of the stage.

"Quick! Places, everyone!" hissed Mr. Hill.

The children crowded into the wings of the stage and Mr. Hill signaled to Joe's classmates Ben and Simon, who were in charge of props and scenery, to open the curtains.

"Good evening, ladies and gentlemen," boomed Mr. Hill, squinting in the glare of the spotlight. "Welcome to the sixth-grade talent show!" There was a loud round of applause.

Joe felt a rush of excitement—he'd never performed in front of people before. He hoped none of their tricks would go wrong.

"I'd like to introduce you to our two judges," continued Mr. Hill.

UNDEAD PETS

"Miss Bruce, sixth-grade teacher, and Mr. Shah, the vice principal."

The judges stood up and gave the audience a wave.

"And now, please welcome our first act, Leonie and Natalie with their recorder duet."

"Earplugs at the ready," Matt said with a giggle.

Leonie scowled at them and flounced on to the stage with Natalie. They launched into

a squeaky performance of "When the Saints Go Marching In."

Joe rolled his eyes and Matt snickered. Mr. Hill glared at them from the other side of the stage so they tried to look serious, but it was tough—especially when Smartie the dog started howling along to "Yankee Doodle"!

As soon as Leonie and Natalie took their bows, Ben ran on and removed the music stand, while Simon dragged Joe and Matt's magic table (which was really a school desk with a shiny tablecloth draped over the top) onto the stage.

Mr. Hill stepped forward. "Please put your hands together for Joe and Matt's mysterious magical mayhem!"

There was an eruption of clapping and a few loud whistles from Matt's dad up front.

Joe and Matt stepped out. There was a whole room full of faces staring back, grinning and clapping.

Joe took a deep breath. "Good evening, ladies and gentlemen . . ." His voice sounded small and tight. He swallowed hard and cleared his throat. "Tonight we'll show you how to make things vanish . . ."

"And reappear!" added Matt, reaching forward and producing a shiny coin from behind Joe's ear.

"Wow!" Toby gasped in the front row.

"Making things appear can be useful," said Joe.

"Especially if you've forgotten your mom's birthday present!" said Matt, whipping out the fake flowers from up his sleeve.

There was another round of applause and more whistles from Matt's dad.

Awwhoooooo . . .

Then Joe pulled the string from his pocket and held it up. "As you can see, there is a knot at the end of this string. But it's easy to make it disappear. All it takes is the magic word . . .

Alakazam!" Joe gave the string a tug, and the knot was gone!

There was a small round of applause and a few grins from the grown-ups who already knew the trick.

"And now, I will bring the knot back!" Joe gathered up the string in his fist and said the magic word again. This time he pulled the other end of the string down and the knot mysteriously reappeared!

Toby's eyes opened wide. "How did they do that?" he called out, looking in admiration at his big brother.

"For our next trick we need a volunteer," called Joe. He was starting to feel confident.

Toby's hand shot up. "Me!"

Matt grinned and called him onstage.

"Take a look inside this top hat," said Matt, holding it in front of Toby. "Check there's nothing inside."

"It's empty," said Toby.

"Not for long!" Joe waved his hands mysteriously above the hat, then pulled out a bright yellow handkerchief . . . and then two more.

"Wow!" Toby beamed.

As the applause died away, Matt continued. "Let's see if the hat's magic will work one more time."

At that moment, the lights flickered and then went out, plunging the hall into darkness. In a blink they came back on again, and Joe saw a white rabbit shoot out of the top hat and land with a thud on the table. But it wasn't the cuddly toy he'd been expecting. It looked almost real.

"Where did you get that rabbit from, Matt?" he whispered.

But Matt didn't seem to have noticed it. He was still digging around inside the top hat. "I can't get the rabbit out. It's jammed!"

Joe frowned. "But Matt . . ." His words trailed off as he looked at the rabbit.

It turned its head and looked directly at Joe. Its eyes were glowing ghoulishly.

"Hi, Joe, my name's Fluffy," the rabbit squeaked. "I've got twenty-four hours to save my owner, and I need your help!"

CHAPTER TWO

Joe's shoulders sagged and he gave a low groan. It was an undead pet! A zombie animal who wanted his help to solve its problems so that it could pass peacefully into the afterlife.

Ever since his uncle Charlie had given him a mysterious Egyptian amulet, Joe had been hounded by undead pets that only he could see. But this was a first—what was he supposed to do about it while he was onstage in the middle of a magic act?

Joe glared at the rabbit, willing her to disappear, but she sat there staring back at him.

UNDEAD PETS

"Got it!" said Matt suddenly and he pulled out a small pink bunny from the top hat.

The audience let out a huge cheer.

"You can take it if you like," said Matt, handing it to Toby, who proudly trotted back to his seat.

Meanwhile, the undead rabbit still sat on the table, her nose twitching and her eyes bulging. Joe shuddered. Now, as he looked more closely, he could see that her white fur was flecked with blood and there were chunks missing from her floppy ears.

UNDEAD PETS

Matt nudged him and Joe realized that it was his turn to speak. "Oh, yes. For our next trick, we need another volunteer."

Hands shot up around the hall and Joe pointed to a lady a few rows back. "We are going to read your mind. Please think of a number between one and ten, but don't tell us what it is . . ."

The lady nodded.

"Now you need to double that number, then add ten to it . . ."

Joe was trying to ignore Fluffy, but she was on the move, hopping across the table toward him.

"Um . . . Please could you divide that number by two . . ." Joe broke off, staring at the rabbit.

The lady nodded, waiting for the next step.

"And then subtract your original number," said Matt, taking over from Joe.

Joe's attention was back on the zombie

rabbit. She was sitting up on her back legs now, peering at him with her head cocked to one side. Joe noticed she had a long scar down her belly.

"Help me, Joe," Fluffy pleaded. "It's a race against time!"

"And now we will read your mind," said Matt to the lady volunteer. He and Joe closed their eyes, then they both called out, "The answer is five!"

"That's right!" said the lady.

The audience gave a cheer, but Joe was distracted again.

Fluffy was glaring at him. "Stop this nonsense and help me!" she demanded.

Joe shook his head and Fluffy's eyes narrowed.

"Now we're going to finish off with some juggling," said Matt.

The boys walked to the front of the stage and began juggling with three balls each. Joe had been practicing the routine for weeks, but now he couldn't concentrate—he kept looking over his shoulder to see what Fluffy was up to. Suddenly there was a loud *thud* as she knocked the top hat off the table!

The audience gasped. Joe dropped his juggling balls. As he bent down to pick them up, he saw that the rabbit had hopped off the table, nosed her way under the brim, and was now inside the hat, making it move across the stage.

Joe made a grab for the hat, but tripped on his long coat and went sprawling.

The audience roared with laughter.

"What are you doing?" whispered Matt.

Joe made another grab for the hat—and reached it!

He lifted it up and there was the rabbit, peering up at him, her green eyes glowing.

"Ready to help me now, Joe?" Fluffy said.

"No!" Joe put the hat on his head and

went to take a bow with Matt.

The audience was going wild, yelling and clapping, and Matt's dad was whistling like a train. The audience loved them!

Joe glanced across at Matt. He was worried his friend would be upset that he'd messed up the act, but Matt just gave him a thumbs-up! Joe sighed with relief and turned to walk offstage. He took a step and felt something squishy underfoot. He glanced down and saw a large piece of zombie-rabbit poo stuck to the front of his shoe.

CHAPTER THREE

"How did you do that hat trick?" asked Matt as soon as they reached the dressing room.

"Well . . . um . . ." Joe pulled open his coat. He felt hot and sweaty. "It was something my . . . grandpa showed me."

"I didn't know your grandpa could do magic tricks! Cool!"

"Um . . . yeah," Joe muttered, scraping the zombie poo off his shoe.

Just then the door banged open and Ben came bounding in. "That was awesome!" he said. "How did you get the hat to move by itself?"

Joe felt his face turn red. He shrugged. "A magician never reveals his secrets."

"Was it wires attached to your sleeves?" asked Ben. "Or a remote-control car inside the hat?"

Joe swallowed hard. "I can't tell you. If I did, the . . . um . . . Magic Circle would make me disappear—forever!"

Matt rolled his eyes. "I'll have to ask your grandpa next time I see him at your house."

"Hey," said Ben. "The twins' dog is about to go on. You've gotta see it!" He dashed out and Joe followed, glad to escape any more questions.

As they ran back along the corridor, Joe kept an eye out for the zombie rabbit. He wasn't sure where she had gone, but he knew she would be back to haunt him soon! He just hoped she'd wait until the show was over . . .

Ruff! Ruff! Ruff!

By the time the boys got back to the auditorium, Smartie and the twins were already onstage. Joe and Matt crowded into the wings with the others to watch. Ava and Molly had set up an obstacle course with low jumps and a tunnel. Everyone cheered as Smartie leaped over the first fence, then dived over the next. She missed the third one, and went under it on her belly instead. Next Ava produced a Hula Hoop for her to jump through. But just then Joe felt something cold and furry brush past his ankles.

"Hello, Joe. I've been looking for you!" Fluffy was crouched at his feet, peering up at him.

Joe ignored her.

"Are you ready to help me now?" she said stubbornly. "I won't go away until you do!"

Joe scowled down at her, but said nothing.

"The clock is ticking." She snuffled. "Every second counts!"

Joe shook his head and pointed to the stage.

"Huh!" snorted Fluffy. "You don't want to help until the silly show is finished? Well, maybe that will be sooner than you think."

Joe turned to look at Fluffy, but just then the lights flickered and went out. When they came back on, the rabbit had gone.

Ava and Molly took a bow and went offstage with Smartie.

"Our next act tonight is the Heathfield Hurricanes!" announced Mr. Hill. The gymnasts cartwheeled onto the stage. They did headstands and handstands, and one girl even did a backflip. Then they started cartwheeling again, moving across the stage, crisscrossing with one another. But suddenly the lights flickered again, and then went out altogether!

There were bangs, thuds, and yelps from the stage as the gymnasts bumped into one another in the darkness. The audience gasped. At the back of the room, a baby started crying. Smartie began to whine. Then a flashlight beam appeared on the stage . . .

UNDEAD PETS

"Don't panic!" said Mr. Hill, shining his flashlight around the hall. "Everyone stay in your seats. It looks like the storm has caused a power outage. If the electricity doesn't come back on in the next five minutes, then I'm afraid we'll have to cancel the rest of the show."

There was a chorus of groans from the children.

"What about our act?" yowled Spiker, who hadn't done his yo-yo tricks yet.

"How can there be a winner?" wailed Leonie.

Mr. Hill sighed. "I'm going to take a look at the fuse box. Miss Bruce, would you step up here and hold down the fort? Meanwhile, everyone please stay in your seats."

As the minutes ticked past, the audience became restless. Mutterings turned into chatter, and more young children in the audience began to cry.

"I wonder what's happened?" said Matt, peering around the curtain to see if he could spot his parents through the gloom.

"I told you," said Nick. "A tornado is probably going to rip off the roof next!"

Molly gave a yelp. "Don't say that!"

Just then, Joe felt something soft flit past his ankles. A flash of white disappeared behind the stage curtain. Joe frowned. He had a feeling that it wasn't the wind that had ruined the show . . .

"Fluffy!" he said under his breath. He was pretty sure this power outage was her doing!

UNDEAD PETS

His older cousin used to have a rabbit, and Joe remembered how it had once chewed through the telephone wires. Could Fluffy have done the same thing to the power cables here at school?

Mr. Hill reappeared on the stage. "Ladies and gentlemen, I'm very sorry, but we'll have to finish the talent show another time. In a moment we'll open the fire doors at the back of the hall and escort you out of the building."

Miss Bruce appeared backstage. "Everyone come with me, please."

As Joe felt his way down the steps, he saw a pair of determined green eyes peering out from under a chair. He knew the zombie rabbit was to blame. He just knew it!

CHAPTER FOUR

As soon as they got home, Joe kicked off his shoes and raced upstairs. He didn't even bother taking off his coat. He threw open his bedroom door and there, sprawled on his bed, was the rabbit, its nose twitching like an express train.

"Hello, Joe."

"It was you, wasn't it?" he growled. "You ruined my school show!"

"Didn't!" said the rabbit stubbornly. "I actually made your act better."

"Huh!" Joe scowled. "Thanks to you, half

my class didn't even get a chance to perform."

"But I needed your help—urgently!"

"How did you do it anyway?"

Fluffy cocked her head angelically, but didn't reply.

"It was a mean thing to do!" Joe said.

"I keep telling you, time is running out!"

"For what?" snapped Joe.

"For us to find the necklace. If we don't, Olivia's going to be in so much trouble!"

"Olivia?" said Joe. "Who's Olivia?" He

puffed out his cheeks in exasperation. Then he sat down on the end of his bed. He'd learned that it was better to deal with the undead pets as fast as possible—before they had a chance to cause too much chaos!

"Okay," he said with a sigh. "So what's this all about?"

Fluffy sat quietly for a moment, the speed of her nose-twitching beginning to slow.

"Olivia was my owner. I'd been with her for three years. She always paid me lots of attention. Feeding me, cleaning my hutch, brushing my coat . . ."

Undead Pets

Joe made a point not to mention that Fluffy's coat—with its bloodstains and ghastly green glow—didn't look too great now . . .

"And she used to tell me everything," Fluffy continued. "Secrets, stories—she even let me play some of her games. But two days ago, one of her games went a bit wrong. Olivia was in the backyard after school, playing dress-up . . . She'd borrowed her big sister's best necklace. She came and showed it to me. She looked like a princess!

"But then, when she was running, the clasp came undone and the necklace fell off into the long grass. Olivia didn't notice it happen. She was too caught up in her game. But I saw it. You see, I like to watch everything that happens in the backyard . . ."

"So, what happened next?" asked Joe. "Did she realize she'd lost the necklace?"

"No," said Fluffy glumly. "I tried to get her attention. I banged my bowl on the bars of my hutch. But she just thought I wanted her to come and see me—which she did. I couldn't tell her what had happened! Then her mom called her into the house."

Joe frowned. "She must have remembered the necklace eventually . . ."

Fluffy nodded. "She came back out later and had a quick look around the yard, so she must have realized it was lost by then, but she couldn't find it. Then I heard her say that she must have lost it in the house, and she went back inside to look for it."

"And what about Olivia's sister? Didn't she realize it was missing?"

Fluffy shook her head. "Not at first. Sally only wore it on special occasions. But yesterday I heard her on her cell phone, telling her friend that she was looking forward to the school dance on Saturday night and how she was planning to wear her necklace."

"Uh-oh!" said Joe.

Undead Pets

Fluffy nodded. "I knew Olivia would get into a lot of trouble when Sally discovered it was missing, so I decided to help her . . ."

The rabbit's nose began twitching faster again and her ears were quivering, too. Then she started to shake.

"Does it have something to do with . . . um . . . how you died?" asked Joe gently.

Fluffy nodded.

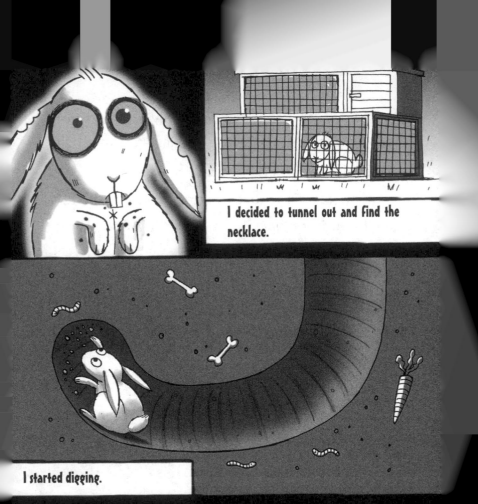

I decided to tunnel out and find the necklace.

I started digging.

It didn't take long.

I began looking for the necklace.

But I didn't spot the fox in the bushes.

"It got you?"

Fluffy nodded, looking down at her big, bulgy scar.

"Ugh!" groaned Joe.

"Olivia's dad found me. He took me to the vet, and they stitched me up. But it was too late." Fluffy stuck out her tongue and made a "corpse" face.

"What about the necklace?" said Joe, trying to change the subject. "Is Olivia still looking for it?"

"She's so sad about me dying, she's forgotten all about it. That's why we need to find it for her. And there's not much time left! The dance is tomorrow, and Olivia's sister will need the necklace when she's getting ready. We have to find it tonight."

"But it's nearly nine o'clock!" said Joe. "It's dark outside. You might be able to see where you're going with those crazy eyes of yours, but I'm just an ordinary human. I can't see in the dark."

UNDEAD PETS

"You've got a flashlight, don't you?"

Fluffy hopped up the length of Joe's bed and lifted the pillow with her teeth, revealing the flashlight he kept underneath. He had no idea how Fluffy knew it was there—he didn't want to think too much about the powers of these strange undead creatures that kept bothering him!

"I can't just go out at night by myself. Mom and Dad will go crazy!"

"Don't be such a wimp—it's just next door!"

Joe's eyes widened. "Olivia lives next door?"

A new family, the Steels, had moved in a few weeks ago. Joe had seen the two daughters but hadn't taken much notice of them.

"Now, listen carefully," said Fluffy. "I heard Sally arranging to meet her friend at seven tomorrow night, which means she'll probably start getting ready at six." Fluffy glanced at Joe's bedroom clock. "That gives us less than twenty-two hours to save Olivia!"

Joe puffed out his cheeks. It was like being briefed for an army rescue mission! "Can't we just wait until the morning?"

"No!" snapped Fluffy. "The family would spot you! It has to be tonight."

Joe thought about it for a moment. It was dark outside, and the wind was howling. But if he wanted to be an explorer like Uncle Charlie, he'd have to get used to stuff like this. Maybe that was why Joe's uncle had given him the amulet in the first place—to test him . . .

"Okay," he said finally. "But we'll need to wait until Mom and Dad are in bed. They'll go ballistic if they see me sneaking outside."

CHAPTER FIVE

Joe shivered as he let himself out through the kitchen door into the backyard. There was no moonlight—it was too cloudy. The only light was from Joe's flashlight and Fluffy's glowing coat.

The rabbit raced down the path and disappeared into the bushes.

Joe tugged down his ski mask and crept after her. He didn't really like wearing the ski mask—it made his head itch—but he knew it was essential to cover as much skin as possible.

That way hopefully no one would spot him.

"Fluffy? Where are you?" He stopped halfway down the lawn.

The tall trees at the bottom of the yard creaked and moaned in the wind, their leaves rustling and their branches banging eerily against the fence. Even everyday things like the clothesline and the swing loomed out of the darkness—big, black, and threatening. The swings moved, too—squeaking as though ghostly children were playing on them.

"Fluffy?" Joe whispered.

"Over here!"

She was waiting by the fence between the Steels' yard and Joe's.

"Want a boost?" said Joe. Without thinking,

he bent down and picked up the rabbit.

"No!" She scrambled to get free, her back claws digging into Joe's hands, giving him a nasty cut across the knuckles.

"*Ow!*" Joe yelped, dropping Fluffy quickly.

"What did you do that for?" Fluffy yelled. "I don't like being picked up. Don't you know anything about rabbits?"

"I know that they're annoying!" Joe replied angrily.

Fluffy glared up at him. "Come on, let's go. And I definitely don't need your help to get over the fence!"

With that, she hopped straight through it as though it didn't exist—unlike Joe, who had to heave himself over. He landed on the other side and rubbed his hand, which was still throbbing from Fluffy's scratch.

"Quick! Over here, Joe! I think this is the place where Olivia lost the necklace." Fluffy was poking around Joe's neighbors' lawn.

UNDEAD PETS

Joe crept over. The grass was long—it hadn't been cut for quite a while, by the look of it. His eyes darted around. It felt wrong to be in someone else's yard, especially at night. He couldn't see any lights on in the Steels' house. He hoped they were all in bed, just like his family. Joe gulped. He felt like a burglar.

"What does the necklace look like?" he whispered.

"It's a thin gold chain with a heart-shaped locket on the end," Fluffy replied.

"And you're sure this is where it fell off?"

"I think so..." Fluffy pushed her nose in a clump of grass and began nibbling a few blades. *"Mmm . . . sweet . . ."*

"Stop snacking and start searching!" said Joe irritably. He shone his flashlight across the lawn, but the grass was so long and thick, it was like looking for a grain of rice on a beach. He crouched down and ran his fingers over the ground. Nothing . . . apart from a few slimy slugs. Joe flicked one off his fingers and wiped the slime on his pants.

"Are you sure this is where she lost it?" Joe asked.

"Well, this was definitely where the fox got me!" said Fluffy.

At that moment, one of Fluffy's ears shot up and her eyes began to glow even brighter than before. Then her nose started twitching at turbo-speed . . .

"Danger!" Fluffy said. She banged the ground with her back leg, making a loud thumping noise.

"What's going on?" whispered Joe. "What

are you doing?" He glanced at the trees. And then the bushes. Was it another fox? "A fox can't hurt you now, Fluffy—you're already dead!"

But it wasn't a fox that had caught Fluffy's attention. A beam suddenly shone in Joe's eyes, and out of the darkness, rough hands grabbed his jacket and shook him.

"Hey!" growled a deep voice. "What do you think you're doing?"

Joe gasped. He was staring into the angry face of a police officer.

CHAPTER SIX

"What are you doing?" snapped the officer, still holding Joe's arm tightly. "Sneaking around, trying to get into the house?"

"Nooooo!" squealed Joe. His mouth went dry. His heart was racing and he felt his legs buckle slightly. "Please . . . My name's Joe Edmunds," he stammered. "I-I live next door!"

"What?" The policeman relaxed his hold on Joe's arm a bit. "Take off your ski mask!"

Joe did as he was told, and the policeman shone a light in Joe's face. Then he sighed.

UNDEAD PETS

"What are you doing in my yard?"

"Your yard?" said Joe. He looked into the man's face. Then he realized that the policeman must be Mr. Steel, his new neighbor! "I-I didn't know you were in the police," Joe stammered.

"Obviously not," said Mr. Steel coldly. "But even if I wasn't in the police, you shouldn't be in my yard in the middle of the night. What are you up to?"

"Well . . ." Joe desperately tried to think up some story to tell. But he was finding it hard

to speak. He had a horrible knot in his throat and his stomach was churning. "You see . . . I've lost something in your yard and I was . . . um . . . looking for it."

"What?"

"Golf balls!" said Joe nervously. It was the first thing he could think of. He hated lying—it always showed on his face. But with a bit of luck, Mr. Steel might not notice in the dark.

"Why were you looking for golf balls in my yard?"

"Well, I was practicing yesterday with my dad's clubs, and I lost a few balls over your fence. They're his best ones—really expensive ones. I wanted to get them back before he noticed."

Mr. Steel let go of Joe's arm and shone the flashlight around the lawn. "I don't see any golf balls . . ."

Joe swallowed hard.

"Mind you," said Mr. Steel with a slight

smile, "the grass is so long, it would be hard to find anything out here!" Then he shone the flashlight back at Joe. "Come on. Let's go and see what your dad thinks about all this."

Joe groaned. He knew exactly what his dad would think about it. He'd be grounded forever—at least until he was forty-two!

Mr. Steel led him down the gravel path at the side of the house, around to Joe's front door.

"How did you get over the fence?" asked Mr. Steel. "Must have been a bit of a climb!"

Joe kept his head down and didn't reply. His heart was still racing. He'd never been in this much trouble before.

As they stood outside Joe's house, waiting for his parents to answer the doorbell, Mr. Steel yawned. "We should both be in bed, Joe!"

Joe nodded glumly. He felt ridiculous standing on his own doorstep, dressed like a burglar with a policeman by his side!

"What's going on?" asked Dad, opening the door in his bathrobe. He glanced at Joe and then at the policeman. "What in the world have you done, Joe?"

"I'm afraid I found your boy in my yard," said Mr. Steel. "Says he was looking for golf balls . . ."

"What?" Then it dawned on Dad who the policeman was. "It's Mr. Steel, isn't it?" he said.

"I'm so sorry. Please come in."

"No, I won't, thanks very much. I've just got back from work and there's a cup of tea waiting for me in the kitchen." He smiled at Joe. "Though it's probably a bit cold by now."

"I can't tell you how embarrassed I am," said Dad. "We've been meaning to come over and introduce ourselves. This wasn't quite what I had in mind!" He glared at Joe. "I hope you've apologized for going into Mr. Steel's yard."

"I'm really sorry, honestly I am." Joe scuffed the floor.

Mr. Steel shrugged. "Let's say nothing more about it. I was a kid once myself, Joe. And I know that boys sometimes have crazy ideas."

"That's very nice of you!" said Dad. "Much nicer than Joe deserves!"

As soon as the door closed, his dad exploded. "How could you be so stupid! Sneaking out in the middle of the night and trespassing in our new neighbor's yard—our new neighbor who is a police sergeant! Of all the ridiculous things to do!"

Joe hung his head.

"And looking for golf balls? I don't even play golf! What do you think you were doing?"

"Well . . . I . . ."

"Was it some sort of spy prank or something?"

Joe nodded. "Yeah, something like that."

"Well, that's not okay, Joe! First thing tomorrow you're going over to Mr. Steel's house to apologize properly . . ."

Joe nodded. He felt tears welling up in his eyes. "I'm really sorry. I'll never do it again."

"You most certainly won't! You're grounded!"

"What's going on?" Mom had appeared on the landing. "Who was at the door? Joe, what are you doing in your clothes?"

"He's been outside sneaking around the neighbor's yard!"

"Oh, Joe!" said Mom. Suddenly she sneezed four times in a row like a cat choking on a hair ball.

"Get to bed!" Dad growled at Joe. "We'll talk about this again in the morning." He stomped upstairs and Joe followed behind. On the landing he could see a glowing green shape—Fluffy was lurking behind the laundry basket.

"What happened?" His big sister, Sarah, poked her head out her bedroom door. "What's Freak Boy done now?"

"Don't call him that!" snapped Mom. Then her nose twitched, and suddenly she was off again, sneezing like a twenty-one-gun salute. Fluffy's fur was sending her allergies into overdrive!

"Tell me!" shouted Sarah, just loud enough to be heard above Mom's nose. "What did he do now?"

"Your brother decided to pay the new

neighbors a visit," Dad answered. "Only he went dressed like a burglar in the middle of the night—without an invitation!"

Sarah's eyes widened. "You're kidding, right?"

"No, I'm not kidding."

Joe scowled at his sister.

Her face lit up like a Halloween pumpkin. "Just wait till I tell my friends . . ."

"Shut up!" growled Joe.

"Bed! Now! Both of you," said Mom, in between sneezes.

Joe slunk to his room. As he passed Toby's door, his brother stuck out his head.

"You're awesome, Joe!" Toby whispered, then he ducked back into his room before Dad could scold him, too.

CHAPTER SEVEN

"So, what do we do now?" Fluffy was already waiting in his room, sitting on his bedside table next to the clock.

"Nothing!" Joe replied, flicking off his shoes and hoping one might accidentally bop Fluffy on the head. "I'm not going out again."

"But you have to! Look at the clock, Joe. We've got less than nineteen hours left—every second counts! You've got to help me find that necklace."

"No!" This time Joe deliberately flung a

sock at the rabbit, but she ducked. "Get lost!" he growled. "I've had enough of you . . . and your problems." He pulled on his pajamas and crawled into bed.

Fluffy glared silently at him for a few minutes, then she sat back on her large hind legs and began cleaning herself, sending clumps of fur flying. It made the room look like a blizzard.

"Stop that!" Joe spluttered. The fluff was getting up his nose and into his throat. He coughed a few times and spat out some hair.

"Help me, Joe!" said Fluffy. "Please . . . ? Now!"

"No!" Joe dived under the covers. "GO AWAY!" he yelled.

Joe waited a few moments, then peeked

out from under the comforter. The rabbit had gone. But her fur hadn't. Joe got out of bed and opened the window, hoping some might blow away. Then he dived back under his covers.

DING-DONG! DING-DONG!

Joe opened his eyes and groaned. His throat was dry, and his hand throbbed where Fluffy had clawed him. He glanced at his clock. It was six in the morning.

DING-DONG!

Joe frowned. Who was ringing the doorbell at this hour? And then suddenly it hit him. The community tag sale! He was supposed to be helping Matt and his mom.

He jumped out of bed and yanked open the curtains. Outside, he could see Matt's mom in her car, waving up at him.

DING-DONG! DING-DONG! Matt was

ringing the doorbell again.

"Pants!" muttered Joe. He turned to get dressed and stepped straight into a pile of slimy rabbit plops. "Ugh!" He grimaced.

"Joe?" His mom appeared at the bedroom door.

Joe panicked, wondering how he was going to explain the rabbit droppings all over the bedroom floor. Then he remembered that only he could see them.

"I'd forgotten about the—" His mom sneezed "—tag sale! Matt and his mom are here already!" She sneezed another six times, sounding like a steam train setting off from a station. "I don't know what's wrong with me," she added.

"Maybe it was Smartie, the twins' dog," said Joe, pulling on a sweatshirt. "I was petting her a bit at the show. Maybe some dog hairs got stuck on my clothes."

"Where do you think you're going?" snapped Dad, who had appeared in the doorway next to Mom. "You're grounded, remember!"

"But it's the big tag sale!" squeaked Joe. "Matt and I are helping out, remember . . ."

"I don't care," said Dad. "After last night's nonsense, you're not going anywhere!"

DING-DONG! DING-DONG!

"I'll get the door!" called Toby, who'd appeared at the top of the stairs in his pajamas.

"Tell them Joe's not coming!" said Dad as Toby dashed downstairs.

"But it's not Stephanie's fault," Mom said to Dad. She was good friends with Matt's mom, Stephanie. "When I saw her at the show last night, she mentioned how grateful she is that Joe and Matt are helping her."

"And Matt and I have been sorting out

loads of our old stuff to sell," added Joe with a pleading look on his face. "Please, Dad."

"I think we should let him go," said Mom, pinching her nose to try and stop the sneezing.

Dad frowned. "Fine. But don't think you're off the hook, Joe. Not by any means."

Joe nodded.

"Grab a juice box and some fruit for the car," called Mom as Joe raced down the stairs.

"Hi," he said to Matt, who was standing on the doorstep. "I'll just be a minute."

As soon as he went into the kitchen, Fluffy appeared.

"At last! Are you coming outside to help me look for the necklace?" she squeaked, her ears twitching. "I've been looking all night, but I still haven't found it. I need your help!"

Joe shook his head. He grabbed an apple and took a bite out of it, then shoved a juice box into his pocket. "Matt and I are doing a tag sale this morning," he said, taking another bite.

"What?"

"Yeah, I'd forgotten about it," he whispered, so Matt wouldn't hear. "But I'll be back by lunchtime."

Fluffy glanced at the kitchen clock. It was 6:15 a.m. "But we've got less than twelve hours! How am I supposed to find the necklace by myself?"

"Maybe it's not there," said Joe, taking another bite of apple. "Maybe a hedgehog ate it! Or a bird flew off with it!"

"No! It's there, I saw her lose it! We just have to find it," said Fluffy. "Olivia will be in big trouble if we don't."

"What? Like the trouble I got into last night?" Joe rolled his eyes. "Well, if she does get into trouble, she'll survive. And anyway—that's what she gets for stealing her sister's stuff!"

"She didn't steal it, she borrowed it!"

"Come on, Joe!" Matt called from the hall.

Joe stepped over Fluffy and headed out of the kitchen.

But Fluffy hopped after him. "If you don't help me, I'll haunt you forever!"

Joe paused. He could do without a lifetime of zombie-rabbit poop in his bedroom. Not to mention his mom's constant sneezing. What sort of chaos could Fluffy cause if she came to school with him every day? But there was no time to help her now.

"There you are, Joe," said his mom, who

was talking to Matt in the hall. "Hurry up! Don't keep Stephanie waiting any longer."

Joe picked up one of the cardboard boxes full of stuff to sell and Matt picked up the other.

While Matt headed off to the car, Joe's mom reached over and gave him a kiss on the cheek. "I wish I was coming, too! I love all the things you can find at tag sales!"

Suddenly Joe had an idea. As he headed outside, he beckoned Fluffy to follow him. "Bye, Mom," he called.

Halfway to the car, he crouched down and pretended to retie his shoelace. "Listen, Fluffy," he whispered. "Why don't we see if we can find another necklace at the tag sale?"

The rabbit sat up on her back legs, her eyes blinking and her nose twitching. "What do you mean?"

"There's lots of stuff at tag sales. We could find a necklace that looks just like Sally's!"

UNDEAD PETS

"Really?" Fluffy didn't sound convinced.

Joe shrugged. "I don't know! But it's worth a try."

"You'd better be right, Joe. Otherwise, I'm your new pet!" Fluffy's eyes bulged and her teeth poked out in a ghastly grimace.

Joe shivered. He definitely didn't want to see that face every day.

CHAPTER EIGHT

The community tag sale was in a large field just out of town. By the time they got there, there was already a long line of cars waiting to park and start selling.

Joe was in the backseat with his boxes next to him. But he wasn't alone. Fluffy was crouching in the backseat, her green eyes glaring up at Joe from the darkness.

"Did you put those toy trains in?" asked Matt, leaning over from the front seat. "And the tracks they go with?"

"No, Toby nabbed them. But I've got loads of old comic books. And some games, a few jigsaw puzzles, some old Halloween costumes . . ."

"Not that old cowboy outfit!" Matt grinned. "You used to wear that to parties."

"Yeah—like you and that yellow fireman's helmet! You even used to wear it to the store."

"No, I didn't!"

"Yes, you did," said Matt's mom. "You thought you were a real firefighter. You were always asking if anyone needed rescuing!"

They found a parking spot, and Joe and Matt helped Stephanie set up two long tables, one on either side of the car.

"You boys can have that one, and I'll put my stuff on the other," she said. "And the things I'm selling for Grandma can sit on the trunk."

Fluffy sat underneath the boys' table. "I don't like this place," she whispered. "It's too busy. Too noisy! I want to go home and look for the necklace."

Joe ignored her.

"You've got loads of CDs," said Matt as Joe unpacked one of his boxes. He held up a CD. "What's this one? *Slumber Party Sleepy Songs!*"

"That's Sarah's," said Joe, snatching the CD from his friend. "And so is that one." He snatched another CD that Matt was waving around.

"*Brownie Campfire Tunes* doesn't sound like your thing, Joe."

UNDEAD PETS

"Sarah's always leaving her junk in my room—there's lots of her old stuff in here," he added.

People were already walking around, looking for deals.

"How much for the comics?" asked an old couple.

"Five bucks for all of them!" said Joe hopefully.

They didn't haggle. But others did.

"Ten dollars! Take it or leave it!" said Matt as a grumpy-looking kid tried to get him to drop the price of a large box of toy cars.

"There's a man selling a box over there, and it's only five bucks," said the boy.

"Go and buy his then!" said Joe.

The boy made a face and handed over the ten dollars.

"What about the necklace?" wailed Fluffy from under the table. "When are we going to see if there's another one that looks like it?"

Joe crouched down, pretending to retie his shoelace again. "Soon," he whispered. "Now be quiet!"

"What a nice toy pony!" said an older woman.

Matt snickered. Joe's face turned red.

"My granddaughter would love that," she said. "How much?"

Joe shrugged. "A dollar?"

A girl bought some of the CDs, and a young couple pushing a cart took a pile of jigsaw puzzles.

As the tables began to empty, Matt's mom suggested the boys go off to have a look around. "Just try not to come back with more junk!" she grinned. "Remember, we're trying to get rid of it!"

"Wait for me!" Fluffy hopped out from under the table, her eyes wide and her nose still twitching like mad.

There were hundreds of tables to choose from. Most people sold a bunch of different things—books, CDs, children's clothes, pots, pans, cutlery—while others seemed to specialize in something—one person had only baby clothes, and another sold bikes. One person even seemed to have nothing but ugly ornaments—brown vases, glass bowls, animal figurines . . .

Fluffy zigzagged across the path, darting

from underneath one table to the next.

"Where are the necklaces?" she squeaked.

But Joe was too busy looking at everything to listen to her.

"Yuck!" said Matt as he spotted a particularly ugly pink china ballerina.

"I can't see anything I want," said Joe, dodging around an exercise bike that two men were trying to fit into the backseat of their car.

Then suddenly he saw it. "Look, Matt—over there!" Joe had spotted something that he'd always wanted . . .

"What is it?" said Matt.

"A metal detector!"

"What?"

Joe raced over and picked it up out of the box. It was black and gray with a long handle and a flat disk at the bottom. "Wow, it's got earphones and everything."

"Stop wasting time!" squealed Fluffy, head-butting Joe's ankles angrily.

UNDEAD PETS

"My uncle Charlie used to have one of these," Joe said. "He told me he used it to find arrowheads and old coins."

"Yeah," said the man selling it. "It's a great thing to have—especially if your mom loses her wedding ring. You'll be a hero, kid!"

UNDEAD PETS

Joe was examining the metal detector carefully, not paying much attention to the man. Then Joe realized what he had just said.

He stopped and thought for a moment. A slow smile spread across his face. Of course! He could use the metal detector to find the necklace! "How much?" he asked.

"Twenty dollars!"

Joe pulled the money out of his pocket and counted it up carefully. "I've got twelve."

The man shook his head.

"Want to split it?" he asked Matt.

"Dunno . . . I've never thought about buying one before."

"Watch this," the man said. He dropped a penny on the ground (just missing Fluffy's nose) and turned on the metal detector. "Listen!" As he wafted it over the coin, the machine let out a loud, high-pitched whine. "You'll be digging up gold in no time if you buy this."

Fluffy gave a shriek. "I don't like that noise!"

Matt grinned. "Awesome! I've only got six bucks, though."

"Would you take eighteen?" said Joe.

"Okay," the man answered with a smile.

Just then, there was a loud chime from a clock sitting on one of the nearby tables. "Look at the time!" Fluffy squealed. "It's already noon. We've only got six hours left! We've got to go, Joe!"

CHAPTER NINE

"Want to come back to my house to try out the metal detector?" asked Matt as his mom drove them out of the field and back onto the road.

"No!" squeaked Fluffy, who was sitting by Joe's feet, fidgeting and hopping from one side of the car to the next.

"I can't," said Joe nervously. "I'm sort of grounded . . ."

"Why?" asked Matt.

Joe took a deep breath. He definitely

didn't want to tell Matt that he'd been caught sneaking around his neighbor's yard in the middle of the night—especially not after all the weird stuff that had happened during their magic act.

"I . . . sort of . . . lost a ball in the neighbor's yard, and went looking for it without asking."

"Make her drive faster!" squeaked Fluffy.

A little cloud of zombie-rabbit fluff drifted

up and tickled Joe's nose. He sniffed and tried not to sneeze.

"Want to come over to my house tomorrow, instead?" asked Joe. "Then we can try out the metal detector in my backyard?"

"Sure!"

"Maybe I should take the metal detector for now and make sure the batteries are charged," said Joe. "Would that be okay?"

Matt shrugged. "Sure."

Matt's mom flicked on the radio—the one o'clock news was starting . . .

Fluffy jumped onto Joe's lap. "Come on, Joe! Only five hours left—it's an emergency!"

Joe felt something wet and cold dribble down his legs. He grimaced. Fluffy had just peed on him!

As soon as Joe opened the door, Fluffy raced out of the car and scampered up the Steels' driveway.

UNDEAD PETS

Joe grabbed the metal detector and headed for his backyard. He spotted his dad doing some weeding in one of the flower beds. Sarah was there, too, lounging on the grass, reading a magazine.

"Well, if it isn't my baby brother, the burglar!"

"Get lost, Sarah!" Joe shot her a scowl.

"That's enough, both of you!" said Dad. "Have you come to help me, Joe?"

"Yeah," he mumbled, casting a quick look over the Steels' fence to see what was happening. If no one was around, maybe he could sneak over and try out the metal detector.

"What's that you've got there?" Dad straightened up from his weeding.

"It's a metal detector. Matt and I bought it at the tag sale."

"I used to have one of those. Let me see."

Joe handed it over and then glanced across the fence again. He could see Mr. Steel over in his backyard.

"I told Mr. Steel you'd be over to apologize properly when you got back," Dad said. "You can stop by after he's cut the grass."

"What?" Joe gasped. *The grass!* If Mr. Steel was about to mow the lawn, he'd mangle the necklace for sure!

"And you could offer to do some work for him," said Dad. "A couple of hours of weeding

or digging should make up for last night's nonsense!"

Joe didn't mind offering to help. He had bigger problems. How was he going to stop Mr. Steel from cutting the grass? He glanced over the fence again . . . "Maybe I could cut the grass for him?" he suggested.

Dad shook his head. "You're not old enough to use the lawnmower, Joe."

"Yeah, you'd probably chop off your own feet," Sarah said with a giggle.

UNDEAD PETS

"Shut up!" Joe growled.

"Stop it, both of you!" said Dad. "There'll be plenty of other jobs you can do, don't worry!"

At that moment, Mr. Steel appeared at the fence.

"Hello, there," he called. "Don't suppose I could borrow your mower, could I? The mice seem to have gotten to mine!" He held up a chewed cable and grinned.

Joe tried not to laugh. That looked like Fluffy's work!

"Sorry," said Joe's dad. "My father-in-law's borrowed mine. I won't get it back until next week."

"That's a shame," said Mr. Steel. "I promised Kate I'd get the yard under control today!"

"We can always try replacing the cable," said Dad. "I had to do it to ours once before. I think I've still got a spare in the garage. Want to come over and take a look?"

"That would be great, thanks. It looks like I won't have time to do the weeding, at this rate."

"I could do it!" said Joe.

A look of shock passed over his dad's face.

"I mean, while you and my dad fix the mower," stammered Joe, "maybe I could do some weeding for you . . ."

"Really?" Mr. Steel looked slightly suspicious. "That's very . . . neighborly of you, Joe."

"To make up for last night," said Joe, his face now crimson.

CHAPTER TEN

"Tell me again where she lost it," said Joe.

He was up to his ankles in the long grass, and he figured he had ten minutes to find the necklace before Mr. Steel got back from his dad's garage. Joe's dad was good at fixing things. He was a central-heating engineer—he spent his days repairing people's boilers, and he could fix most things.

"I think it was over here," said Fluffy, poking her nose into a clump of grass. "But it might have been over there . . . All the grass looks the same." She sighed with frustration.

Joe grabbed his metal detector and turned it on. "I'll use the headphones so no one will hear." He glanced at the Steels' house. "Keep a lookout and tell me if anyone's coming."

Joe got to work. The metal detector was quite heavy. It made a low humming sound as he wafted it over a patch of grass . . .

Nothing.

He moved over a bit and tried another area . . .

Still nothing.

"Hurry up, Joe!" said Fluffy, peering at Joe's watch. "Look at the time! It's nearly two o'clock now . . . Just four hours left!"

Not only was time running out to find the necklace, but any minute now Mr. Steel would be back, and then the hunt would definitely be over. He'd be stuck with Fluffy forever! He grimaced.

"Keep looking!" squeaked Fluffy.

"I am!" He moved on to another patch of grass. Nothing . . .

"Maybe that thing doesn't work!" said Fluffy irritably.

Joe tried to ignore her. He wafted the detector over a larger area, sweeping it left and right, desperately hoping to hear the high-pitched noise. "The grass is too long!" he grumbled.

"I can hear your dad's voice," said Fluffy. "They're coming back . . ."

She vanished through the fence while Joe moved over to another patch of grass.

"Still nothing!" he groaned. He moved on to another section.

"Quick, Joe! They're coming!" called Fluffy, reappearing through the fence.

"Just a few minutes more . . ." Joe swept the detector even wider.

Then suddenly he felt a hand on his back!

"Argh!" He jumped.

"What are you doing?" A small girl with short brown hair was peering at him. "Are you Joe?" She smiled. "I saw you out of the window."

"Yeah . . ."

"Dad told me about you." She giggled. "What are you doing?"

"Looking for treasure?" Joe said nervously.

"Me too," said the girl, frowning. "I'm looking for a necklace. I lost it. I thought it was in the house, but I can't find it." Her lip began to wobble, and for an awful moment Joe thought she might be about to cry.

"Well, maybe I can look for it, too?" said Joe. "Maybe it's out here . . ."

"What's that?" She pointed at the metal detector.

"It finds stuff," said Joe.

"Can I try it?"

Fluffy gave a squeal. "They're coming, Joe! Quick!"

Joe swept the detector over yet another patch of grass. If only the thing would work!

"Let me do it," said Olivia, reaching for the handle.

But just then there was a high-pitched whine from the detector . . .

Joe felt a surge of hope.

Fluffy gave a squeal.

UNDEAD PETS

Olivia's eyes widened. "What is it?" she asked.

Joe squatted down and ran his hand through the grass. Where was it? Then he saw something shine. He reached forward and grabbed it.

"It's just a bottle cap," said Olivia.

Joe held the cap in the palm of his hand. He kneeled down on the grass and sighed. He'd never find it now! He was just about to stand up when he felt something hard under his left knee. He rocked back on his heels and parted the grass . . .

"The necklace!" squealed Olivia.

There it was. A thin gold chain and locket, embedded in the mud.

Joe dug it out with his fingernails and handed it to Olivia. She clutched it to her chest and beamed at him.

Undead Pets

"What are you doing, Joe?"

He spun around to find Mr. Steel and his dad standing there.

"Joe's looking for treasure!" Olivia grinned.

Joe noticed she'd tucked the necklace safely out of sight, behind her back.

"I was just showing Olivia my metal detector. Sorry . . . I'll get back to the weeding now." Joe slunk back to the flower beds, dragging his metal detector with him.

Fluffy was already waiting there. "You did it, Joe!"

Joe glanced behind him to make sure no one was watching. Olivia had already disappeared back into the house—to return the necklace, Joe guessed. Mr. Steel and Joe's dad were testing out the mower.

"Thanks for everything, Joe. I can pass over happily now. By the way, Olivia's a nice girl . . . I think you two are going to be the best of friends. In fact"—Fluffy chuckled—"I'm sure of it . . ."

"What? What do you mean?" Joe didn't like the sound of that. He definitely didn't want to be best friends with a six-year-old girl! But Fluffy had already begun to fade.

"Good-bye, Joe! Thanks again!"

"Wait! What do you mean about Olivia and me being friends?" Joe called out to the rabbit.

But Fluffy was disappearing.

A moment later, she was gone, leaving nothing but a few clumps of fur that blew away in the breeze.

"Hello, Joe?"

Joe jumped. Olivia had reappeared behind him. He gulped. Had she heard him talking to Fluffy?

"Can we look for treasure again?" she asked. "And can we walk to school together on Monday? Dad says it's okay."

"Huh?"

Joe glanced up and Mr. Steel gave him a

wave from the other end of the yard.

Was it Joe's imagination, or was Mr. Steel smirking?

"It's great to have a special friend next door!" Olivia said, beaming.

For one terrible moment, Joe thought she was about to kiss him. He backed away and fell over the metal detector.

"I think I better go," he said, picking the metal detector up and holding it out in front of him like a barrier. "Mom's calling me . . ."

"No, she isn't!" Olivia's bottom lip began to wobble.

Joe raced out of the yard.

As he ran, a bird swooped low, missing his head by inches. It didn't look like any bird he'd seen in the neighborhood before. He glanced around, but it had gone. There was a feather lying on the path in front of him . . . a bright green feather!

Joe was just an ordinary boy
until he made a wish on a
spooky Egyptian amulet.
Now he's the Protector of
UNDEAD PETS . . . and there's
a pesky parakeet flapping around!

Pete had a run-in with a window and lost.
Now the zombie parakeet needs Joe's help
so he can fly to his final destination!

Joe was just an ordinary boy
until he made a wish on a
spooky Egyptian amulet.
Now he's the Protector of
UNDEAD PETS ... and there's a
ravenous rodent on the rampage!

Dumpling the hamster got sucked up a vacuum
cleaner. Can Joe help him sort out his unfinished
business, so he can finally bite the dust?

Joe was just an ordinary boy
until he made a wish on a
spooky Egyptian amulet.
Now he's the Protector of
UNDEAD PETS ... and there's
a crazy cat on his tail!

Poor Pickle met her end under the wheels of a car.
Can Joe help Pickle protect her sister before
there's another catastrophe?

Joe was just an ordinary boy
until he made a wish on a
spooky Egyptian amulet.
Now he's the Protector of
UNDEAD PETS ... and there's a
demented dog off the leash!

Dexter chased a squirrel right off the edge
of a cliff. Can Joe help him give up the ghost
once and for all?

Joe was just an ordinary boy
until he made a wish on a
spooky Egyptian amulet.
Now he's the Protector of
UNDEAD PETS ... and there's a
ghoulish goldfish making a splash!

Fizz the goldfish got flushed.
Can Joe help him take revenge so
he can go belly-up forever?